HEALING SCRIPTURES

ALSO BY JOSEPH PRINCE

Eat Your Way to Life and Health

No More Mind Games

Anchored

Thoughts for Let-Go Living

Live the Let-Go Life

The Prayer of Protection

Grace Revolution

The Power of Right Believing

Unmerited Favor

Destined to Reign

Health and Wholeness Through the Holy Communion

The Benjamin Generation

Spiritual Warfare

For more information on these books and other inspiring resources, visit JosephPrince.com.

JOSEPH PRINCE

HEALING SCRIPTURES

POWERFUL PROMISES FOR DIVINE HEALTH

Cover design by 22 Media Pte Ltd.

Unless otherwise noted, Scripture quotations are taken from the King James Version of the Bible.

All italics in Scripture quotations were added by the author for emphasis.

Healing Scriptures—Powerful Promises for Divine Health

ISBN 978-981-14-1760-3

Joseph Prince Resources

JosephPrince.com

Printed in the Republic of Singapore

First edition

CONTENTS

INTRODUCTION

My dear friend, I'm so glad to be able to get this resource into your hands and to give you a compilation of powerful healing promises to meditate on.

As you go through these scriptures, I pray that you will see how much our Lord Jesus loves you and how He wants you and your loved ones living a long, good, and healthy life.

Today whether you just want to experience a greater measure of health and life, or you are battling a serious medical condition, or trusting the Lord for a healing breakthrough for someone you love, can I encourage you to give priority to His Word? Just take a look at what happens when you find His words and meditate on them:

> My son, *give attention to my words;* incline your ear to my sayings. Do not let them depart from your eyes; *keep them in the midst of your heart; for they are life to those who find them, and health to all their flesh.* (Prov. 4:20–22 NKJV)

The Word of God is life and health to *all* your flesh. This means there is no part of your flesh that His Word will not touch with its life-giving and healing properties.

Just think about that.

I give thanks for medicine—it has helped so many people. But while medicine may benefit one part of your body, it sometimes harms another part of your body. Only the Word of God is health to *all* your flesh—your eyes, your pancreas, your kidneys, your prostate, your heart, your skin, your bones . . . to *every* part of you!

I can't wait for this to become your reality. This is why I've put together some everlasting promises on healing in this scriptural companion to my book on the holy Communion *Eat Your Way to Life and Health*.

With specially designed features, I believe this resource will help you to meditate more effectively on the Lord's promises for your health and wholeness. I believe these scriptures will speak directly to you, encourage you, and strengthen you. They will flush out your fears, anchor your heart, and release healing into your body. I have also prepared an abridged audio version of this resource where I read selected healing scriptures, and it is now available on our resource store at JosephPrince.com/healing.

Beloved, as you garrison your heart with the living Word, may they cause you to run to our Lord Jesus and begin to lay hold of the healing and divine life that are your blood-bought blessings in Christ.

I'm believing that as you read and meditate on His words of life in the following pages, you will see the living, active, and powerful Word of God putting an end to your days of sickness and weakness.

I also want to encourage you to go into the Word yourself if you can. I personally love reading the accounts of Jesus' healing miracles in the gospels. As you meditate on healing scriptures and keep your eyes on your Healer, I'm believing that there will be such an impartation of faith and life that you will experience breakthroughs of healing, rejuvenation, and restoration. Amen!

OLD TESTAMENT SCRIPTURES

The word of the LORD came unto Abram in a vision, saying, Fear not, Abram: I am thy shield, and thy exceeding great reward.

GENESIS 20:17 NASB

Abraham prayed to God, and God healed Abimelech and his wife and his maids, so that they bore children.

EXODUS 12:13

When I see the blood, I will pass over you, and the plague shall not be upon you to destroy you.

And Moses said to the people, "Do not be afraid. Stand still, and see the salvation of the LORD, which He will accomplish for you today. For the Egyptians whom you see today, you shall see again no more forever. The LORD will fight for you, and you shall hold your peace."

EXODUS 15:2 NASB

The LORD is my strength and song, and He has become my salvation; this is my God, and I will praise Him.

EXODUS 15:26

I am the LORD that healeth thee.

EXODUS 23:25–26 NASB

But you shall serve the LORD your God, and He will bless your bread and your water; and I will remove sickness from your midst. There shall be no one miscarrying or barren in your land; I will fulfill the number of your days.

DEUTERONOMY 7:14–15 NASB

You shall be blessed above all peoples; there will be no male or female barren among you or among your cattle. The LORD will remove from you all sickness; and He will not put on you any of the harmful diseases of Egypt which you have known.

That your days may be multiplied, and the days of your children, in the land which the LORD sware unto your fathers to give them, as the days of heaven upon the earth.

DEUTERONOMY 30:19–20 NASB

I call heaven and earth to witness against you today, that I have set before you life and death, the blessing and the curse. So choose life in order that you may live, you and your descendants, by loving the LORD your God, by obeying His voice, and by holding fast to Him; for this is your life and the length of your days, that you may live in the land which the LORD swore to your fathers, to Abraham, Isaac, and Jacob, to give them.

DEUTERONOMY 31:6 NASB

Be strong and courageous, do not be afraid or tremble at them, for the LORD your God is the one who goes with you. He will not fail you or forsake you.

DEUTERONOMY 33:25

As thy days, so shall thy strength be.

RUTH 4:15

He shall be unto thee a restorer of thy life, and a nourisher of thine old age.

I KINGS 5:4 NASB

But now the LORD my God has given me rest on every side; there is neither adversary nor misfortune.

I KINGS 8:56 NASB

Blessed be the LORD, who has given rest to His people Israel, according to all that He promised; not one word has failed of all His good promise, which He promised through Moses His servant.

JOB 33:24–25 NASB

Then let him be gracious to him, and say, "Deliver him from going down to the pit, I have found a ransom"; let his flesh become fresher than in youth, let him return to the days of his youthful vigor.

JOB 42:12, 16–17

The Lord blessed the latter end of Job more than his beginning. . . . After this lived Job an hundred and forty years, and saw his sons, and his sons' sons, even four generations. So Job died, being old and full of days.

He shall be like a
tree planted by the
rivers of water, that
bringeth forth his
fruit in his season;
his leaf also shall
not wither; and
whatsoever he doeth
shall prosper.

PSALM 3:3

But thou, O LORD, art a shield for me; my glory, and the lifter up of mine head.

The LORD is my shepherd; I shall not want. He maketh me to lie down in green pastures: he leadeth me beside the still waters. He restoreth my soul.

PSALM 29:11

The LORD will give strength unto his people; the LORD will bless his people with peace.

PSALM 30:2

O LORD my God, I cried unto thee, and thou hast healed me.

PSALM 32:7 NLT

You are my hiding place; you protect me from trouble. You surround me with songs of victory.

PSALM 56:3 NLT

When I am afraid, I will put my trust in you.

PSALM 34:17–18 NLT

The Lord hears his people when they call to him for help. He rescues them from all their troubles. The Lord is close to the brokenhearted; he rescues those whose spirits are crushed.

PSALM 34:19–20

Many are the afflictions of the righteous: but the Lord delivereth him out of them all. He keepeth all his bones: not one of them is broken.

PSALM 41:3 NLT

The LORD nurses them when they are sick and restores them to health.

PSALM 50:15 NLT

Call on me when you are in trouble, and I will rescue you, and you will give me glory.

PSALM 55:22 NLT

Give your burdens to the LORD, and he will take care of you. He will not permit the godly to slip and fall.

PSALM 56:13 NLT

You have rescued me from death; you have kept my feet from slipping. So now I can walk in your presence, O God, in your life-giving light.

PSALM 91:5–7

Thou shalt not be afraid for the terror by night; nor for the arrow that flieth by day; nor for the pestilence that walketh in darkness; nor for the destruction that wasteth at noonday. A thousand shall fall at thy side, and ten thousand at thy right hand; but it shall not come nigh thee.

PSALM 91:9–10

Because thou hast made the LORD, which is my refuge, even the most High, thy habitation; **there shall no evil befall thee,** neither shall any plague come nigh thy dwelling.

PSALM 91:15–16

He shall call upon me, and I will answer him:
I will be with him in trouble; I will deliver him,
and honour him. With long life will I satisfy him,
and shew him my salvation.

PSALM 92:12, 14 NKJV

The righteous shall flourish like a palm tree. . . .
They shall still bear fruit in old age; they shall be
fresh and flourishing.

PSALM 103:1–5

Bless the LORD, O my soul: and all that is within me, bless his holy name. Bless the LORD, O my soul, and forget not all his benefits: who forgiveth all thine iniquities; who healeth all thy diseases; who redeemeth thy life from destruction; who crowneth thee with lovingkindness and tender mercies; who satisfieth thy mouth with good things; so that thy youth is renewed like the eagle's.

He brought them forth also with silver and gold: and there was **not one feeble person** among their tribes.

PSALM 107:19–20 NASB

Then they cried out to the LORD in their trouble; He saved them out of their distresses. He sent His word and healed them, and delivered them from their destructions.

PSALM 118:17

I shall not die, but live, and declare the works of the LORD.

PSALM 121:4–5 NLT

He who watches over Israel never slumbers or sleeps. The LORD himself watches over you! The LORD stands beside you as your protective shade.

PSALM 127:2

He giveth his beloved sleep.

PROVERBS 4:20–22

My son, attend to my words; incline thine ear unto my sayings. Let them not depart from thine eyes; keep them in the midst of thine heart. For they are life unto those that find them, and health to all their flesh.

PROVERBS 17:22

A merry heart doeth good like a medicine: but a broken spirit drieth the bones.

PROVERBS 18:21

Death and life are in the power of the tongue: and they that love it shall eat the fruit thereof.

ISAIAH 26:3

Thou wilt keep him in perfect peace, whose mind is stayed on thee: because he trusteth in thee.

He giveth power to the faint; and to them that have no might he increaseth strength. Even the youths shall faint and be weary, and the young men shall utterly fall: but they that wait upon the LORD shall renew their strength; they shall mount up with wings as eagles; they shall run, and not be weary; and they shall walk, and not faint.

ISAIAH 41:10–13 NLT

Don't be afraid, for I am with you. Don't be discouraged, for I am your God. I will strengthen you and help you. I will hold you up with my victorious right hand. See, all your angry enemies lie there, confused and humiliated. Anyone who opposes you will die and come to nothing. You will look in vain for those who tried to conquer you. Those who attack you will come to nothing.

For I hold you by your right hand—I, the LORD your God. And I say to you, "Don't be afraid. I am here to help you."

ISAIAH 46:4 NLT

I will be your God throughout your lifetime—until your hair is white with age. I made you, and I will care for you. I will carry you along and save you.

ISAIAH 53:4–5 AMPC

Surely He has borne our griefs (sicknesses, weaknesses, and distresses) and carried our sorrows and pains [of punishment], yet we [ignorantly] considered Him stricken, smitten, and afflicted by God [as if with leprosy]. But He was wounded for our transgressions, He was bruised for our guilt and iniquities; the chastisement [needful to obtain] peace and well-being for us was upon Him, and with the stripes [that wounded] Him we are healed and made whole.

ISAIAH 58:8 NKJV

Your light shall break forth like the morning, your healing shall spring forth speedily, and your righteousness shall go before you; the glory of the LORD shall be your rear guard.

Then the LORD said to me, "You have seen well, for I am watching over My word to perform it."

Blessed is the man that trusteth in the LORD, and whose hope the LORD is. For he shall be as a tree planted by the waters, and that spreadeth out her roots by the river, and shall not see when heat cometh, but her leaf shall be green; and shall not be careful in the year of drought, neither shall cease from yielding fruit.

JEREMIAH 30:17

I will restore health unto thee, and I will heal thee of thy wounds, saith the LORD.

JEREMIAH 32:27

Behold, I am the LORD, the God of all flesh: is there any thing too hard for me?

Behold, I will bring to it
health and healing, and
I will heal them; and
I will reveal to them
an abundance of peace
and truth.

I will feed my flock, and I will cause them to lie down, saith the Lord God. I will seek that which was lost, and bring again that which was driven away, and will bind up that which was broken, and will strengthen that which was sick.

JOEL 2:25 NKJV

I will restore to you the years that the swarming locust has eaten, the crawling locust, the consuming locust, and the chewing locust.

But unto you that fear my name shall the Sun of righteousness arise with healing in his wings.

NEW TESTAMENT SCRIPTURES

And Jesus went about all Galilee, teaching in their synagogues, preaching the gospel of the kingdom, and healing all kinds of sickness and all kinds of disease among the people. Then His fame went throughout all Syria; and they brought to Him all sick people who were afflicted with various diseases and torments, and those who were demon-possessed, epileptics, and paralytics; and He healed them.

MATTHEW 8:2–3 NKJV

And behold, a leper came and worshiped Him, saying, "Lord, if You are willing, You can make me clean." Then Jesus put out His hand and touched him, saying, "I am willing; be cleansed." Immediately his leprosy was cleansed.

When evening had come, they brought to Him many who were demon-possessed. And He cast out the spirits with a word, and healed all who were sick, that it might be fulfilled which was spoken by Isaiah the prophet, saying: "He Himself took our infirmities and bore our sicknesses."

MATTHEW 9:1–2, 6–8 NKJV

So He got into a boat, crossed over, and came to His own city. Then behold, they brought to Him a paralytic lying on a bed. When Jesus saw their faith, He said to the paralytic, "Son, be of good cheer; your sins are forgiven you." . . . Then He said to the paralytic, "Arise, take up your bed, and go to your house." And he arose and departed to his house. Now when the multitudes saw it, they marveled and glorified God.

MATTHEW 9:27–30 NKJV

When Jesus departed from there, two blind men followed Him, crying out and saying, "Son of David, have mercy on us!" And when He had come into the house, the blind men came to Him. And Jesus said to them, "Do you believe that I am able to do this?" They said to Him, "Yes, Lord." Then He touched their eyes, saying, "According to your faith let it be to you." And their eyes were opened.

MATTHEW 14:14 NKJV

And when Jesus
went out He saw
a great multitude;
and He was moved
with compassion
for them, and
healed their sick.

MATTHEW 15:30–31 NKJV

Then great multitudes came to Him, having with them the lame, blind, mute, maimed, and many others; and they laid them down at Jesus' feet, and He healed them. So the multitude marveled when they saw the mute speaking, the maimed made whole, the lame walking, and the blind seeing; and they glorified the God of Israel.

MARK 6:53–56 NKJV

When they had crossed over, they came to the land of Gennesaret and anchored there. And when they came out of the boat, immediately the people recognized Him, ran through that whole surrounding region, and began to carry about on beds those who were sick to wherever they heard He was. Wherever He entered, into villages, cities, or the country, they laid the sick in the marketplaces, and begged Him that they might just touch the hem of His garment. And as many as touched Him were made well.

So Jesus answered and said to them, "Have faith in God. For assuredly, I say to you, whoever says to this mountain, 'Be removed and be cast into the sea,' and does not doubt in his heart, but believes that those things he says will be done, he will have whatever he says. Therefore I say to you, whatever things you ask when you pray, believe that you receive them, and you will have them."

Later He appeared to the eleven as they sat at the table. . . . And He said to them, "Go into all the world and preach the gospel to every creature. He who believes and is baptized will be saved; but he who does not believe will be condemned. And these signs will follow those who believe: In My name they will cast out demons; they will speak with new tongues; they will take up serpents; and if they drink anything deadly, it will by no means hurt them; they will lay hands on the sick, and they will recover."

LUKE 6:19 NKJV

And the whole multitude sought to touch Him, for power went out from Him and healed them all.

LUKE 13:11–13 NKJV

And behold, there was a woman who had a spirit of infirmity eighteen years, and was bent over and could in no way raise herself up. But when Jesus saw her, He called her to Him and said to her, "Woman, you are loosed from your infirmity." And He laid His hands on her, and immediately she was made straight, and glorified God.

JOHN 10:10–11 NKJV

The thief does not come except to steal, and to kill, and to destroy. I have come that they may have life, and that they may have it more abundantly. I am the good shepherd. The good shepherd gives His life for the sheep.

JOHN 14:27 NKJV

Peace I leave with you, My peace I give to you; not as the world gives do I give to you. Let not your heart be troubled, neither let it be afraid.

Now as Peter was traveling through all those regions, he came down also to the saints who lived at Lydda. There he found a man named Aeneas, who had been bedridden eight years, for he was paralyzed. Peter said to him, "Aeneas, Jesus Christ heals you; get up and make your bed." Immediately he got up.

ACTS 14:8–10 NASB

At Lystra a man was sitting who had no strength in his feet, lame from his mother's womb, who had never walked. This man was **listening** to Paul as he spoke, who, when he had fixed his gaze on him and had seen that he had **faith** to be made well, said with a loud voice, "Stand upright on your feet." And he leaped up and began to walk.

ROMANS 4:16–21 NASB

For this reason it is by faith, in order that it may be in accordance with grace, so that the promise will be guaranteed to all the descendants, not only to those who are of the Law, but also to those who are of the faith of Abraham, who is the father of us all, (as it is written, "A FATHER OF MANY NATIONS HAVE I MADE YOU") in the presence of Him whom he believed, even God, who gives life to the dead and calls into being that which does not exist. In hope against hope he believed, so that he might become a father of many nations according to that which had been spoken, "SO SHALL YOUR DESCENDANTS BE." Without becoming weak in faith he contemplated his own body, now as good as dead since he was about a hundred years old, and the deadness of Sarah's womb; yet, with respect to the promise of God, he did not waver in unbelief but grew strong in faith, giving glory to God, and being fully assured that what God had promised, He was able also to perform.

ROMANS 5:17

For if by one man's offence death reigned by one; much more they which receive abundance of grace and of the gift of righteousness shall reign in life by one, Jesus Christ.

ROMANS 8:2, 11

For the law of the Spirit of life in Christ Jesus hath made me free from the law of sin and death. . . . But if the Spirit of him that raised up Jesus from the dead dwell in you, he that raised up Christ from the dead shall also quicken your mortal bodies by his Spirit that dwelleth in you.

What shall we then say to these things? If God be for us, who can be against us? He that spared not his own Son, but delivered him up for us all, how shall he not with him also freely give us all things?

The cup of blessing which we bless, is it not the communion of the blood of Christ? The bread which we break, is it not the communion of the body of Christ?

For though we walk in the flesh, we do not war after the flesh: (for the weapons of our warfare are not carnal, but mighty through God to the pulling down of strong holds;) casting down imaginations, and every high thing that exalteth itself against the knowledge of God, and bringing into captivity every thought to the obedience of Christ.

2 CORINTHIANS 12:9

And he said unto me, My grace is sufficient for thee: for my strength is made perfect in weakness.

Christ redeemed us from the curse of the Law, having become a curse for us—for it is written, "CURSED IS EVERYONE WHO HANGS ON A TREE"—in order that in Christ Jesus the blessing of Abraham might come to the Gentiles, so that we would receive the promise of the Spirit through faith. . . . And if you belong to Christ, then you are Abraham's descendants, heirs according to promise.

EPHESIANS 6:10–12

Finally, my brethren, be strong in the Lord, and in the power of his might. Put on the whole armour of God, that ye may be able to stand against the wiles of the devil. For we wrestle not against flesh and blood, but against principalities, against powers, against the rulers of the darkness of this world, against spiritual wickedness in high places.

PHILIPPIANS 4:6–7 NASB

Be anxious for nothing, but in everything by prayer and supplication with thanksgiving let your requests be made known to God. And the peace of God, which surpasses all comprehension, will guard your hearts and your minds in Christ Jesus.

HEBREWS 4:16

Let us therefore come boldly unto the throne of grace, that we may obtain mercy, and find grace to help in time of need.

HEBREWS 10:23

Let us hold fast the profession of our faith without wavering; (for he is faithful that promised.)

HEBREWS 13:5 AMPC

He [God] Himself has said, I will not in any way fail you nor give you up nor leave you without support. [I will] not, [I will] not, [I will] not in any degree leave you helpless nor forsake nor let [you] down (relax My hold on you)! [Assuredly not!]

HEBREWS 13:8

Jesus Christ the same yesterday, and to day, and for ever.

JAMES 5:14–16

Is any sick among you? Let him call for the elders of the church; and let them pray over him, anointing him with oil in the name of the Lord: and the prayer of faith shall save the sick, and the Lord shall raise him up; and if he have committed sins, they shall be forgiven him. Confess your faults one to another, and pray one for another, that ye may be healed. The effectual fervent prayer of a righteous man availeth much.

I PETER 2:24 NKJV

Himself bore our sins in His own body on the tree, that we, having died to sins, might live for righteousness—by whose stripes you were healed.

I PETER 5:7 AMPC

Casting the whole of your care [all your anxieties, all your worries, all your concerns, once and for all] on Him, for He cares for you affectionately and cares about you watchfully.

I JOHN 4:4 NASB

You are from God, little children, and have overcome them; because greater is He who is in you than he who is in the world.

I JOHN 4:17

Herein is our love made perfect, that we may have boldness in the day of judgment: because **as he is, so are we in this world.**

Beloved, I wish above all things that thou mayest prosper and be in health, even as thy soul prospereth.

REVELATION 12:11

And they overcame him by the blood of the Lamb, and by the word of their testimony.

REVELATION 22:1–3 NASB

Then he showed me a river of the water of life, clear as crystal, coming from the throne of God and of the Lamb, in the middle of its street. On either side of the river was the tree of life, bearing twelve kinds of fruit, yielding its fruit every month; and the leaves of the tree were for the healing of the nations. There will no longer be any curse.

PRAYER FOR HEALING

My friend, whatever your medical situation or challenge, would you pray this prayer with me? (If you are praying for a loved one, just say your loved one's name as appropriate). Say this with me:

Dear Lord Jesus, thank You for Your love for me.

Thank You for showing me in Your Word that You want me healthy and strong and that You are my healer. That You are not just able, but willing to heal me and give me a good, long life.

Whatever challenge I am facing right now, I know it is not too small for Your attention nor too big for Your grace and power.

I see it completely covered by Your perfect and finished work at the cross. And because of the stripes You bore for me, I declare I am healed.

I thank You that as I meditate on Your healing promises, according to Your Word, they are being made life and health to all my flesh.

I declare that Your Word is working powerfully in my body, healing me, protecting me, restoring to me, and invigorating me with Your resurrection life. I thank You that it is also bringing peace, soundness, and strength to my heart, my mind, and my emotions. Amen!

MEDICAL DISCLAIMER

If you are facing a physical or mental health condition, please understand that this book is not meant to take the place of professional medical advice. If you or your loved one has a health concern or an existing medical condition, please do consult a qualified medical practitioner or healthcare provider. We would also advise you to ask and seek the Lord always for His wisdom and guidance regarding your specific health or medical issue and to exercise faith together with godly wisdom in the management of your own physical, mental, and emotional well-being. Do not, on your own accord, disregard any professional medical advice or diagnosis. Please also do not take what has been shared in this book as permission or encouragement to stop taking your medication or going for medical treatment. While we are unable to provide any guarantees and recognize that different individuals experience different results, we continue to stand in faith to believe and affirm the authority and power of God's Word and healing promises with all who believe in the finished work our Lord Jesus has accomplished on the cross.

SALVATION PRAYER

If you would like to receive all that Jesus has done for you and make Him your Lord and Savior, please pray this prayer:

Lord Jesus, thank You for loving me and dying for me on the cross. Your precious blood washes me clean of every sin. You are my Lord and my Savior, now and forever. I believe You rose from the dead and that You are alive today. Because of Your finished work, I am now a beloved child of God and heaven is my home. Thank You for giving me eternal life and filling my heart with Your peace and joy. Amen.

WE WOULD LIKE TO HEAR FROM YOU

If you have prayed the salvation prayer or if you have a testimony to share after reading this book, please tell us about it via JosephPrince.com/testimony.

STAY CONNECTED WITH JOSEPH

Connect with Joseph through these social media channels and receive daily inspirational teachings:

Facebook.com/JosephPrince
Twitter.com/JosephPrince
Youtube.com/JosephPrinceOnline
Instagram: @JosephPrince

FREE DAILY EMAIL DEVOTIONAL

Sign up for Joseph's free daily email devotional at JosephPrince.com/meditate and receive bite-size inspirations to help you grow in grace.

BOOKS BY JOSEPH PRINCE

Eat Your Way to Life and Health

Come boldly to the Lord's Table and receive your healing! Through engaging Bible-based teaching, Joseph Prince unpacks revelation upon revelation about the holy Communion and shows you why partaking of the bread and cup is God's ordained way to release life, health, and healing to your body. Get faith-fueling answers to pertinent questions you've been asking about divine healing and be encouraged by testimonies from those who have been healed through partaking of the Communion. Whatever your health challenge, don't give up. The Lord has made a way for you to eat your way to life and health!

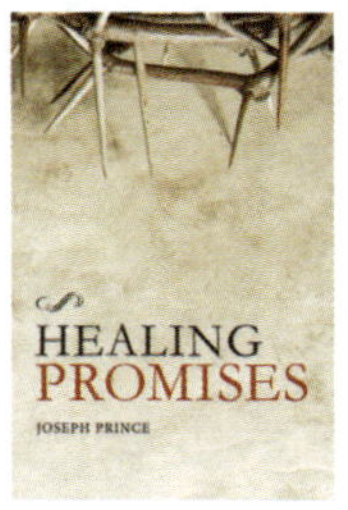

Healing Promises

Healing Promises takes you into the heart of our Lord Jesus and shows you page after page His compassion and willingness to heal you. See from the Word how it's not about what you must do to be healed—it's all about resting in the grace of our Lord, who has done everything for you to be healed. Be encouraged and start walking in a greater measure of health today!

ABOUT THE AUTHOR

JOSEPH PRINCE is a leading voice in proclaiming the gospel of grace to a whole new generation of believers and leaders. He is the senior pastor of New Creation Church in Singapore, a vibrant and dynamic church with a congregation of more than 33,000 attendees. He separately heads Joseph Prince Ministries, a television and media broadcast ministry that is reaching the world with the good news about Jesus' finished work. Joseph is also the bestselling author of *The Power of Right Believing* and *Destined to Reign* and a highly sought-after conference speaker. For more information about his other inspiring resources and his latest audio and video messages, visit JosephPrince.com.